SAVIOURS OF NORDENHEIM

MUHAMMAD OMAR QURESHI

Made with ♥ on the Notion Press Platform
www.notionpress.com

Contents

I

Introduction

Graham was knocked out in his home, snoozing away on his bed before an abrupt ring on his cellphone jolted him awake. The screen glowed brightly in the dark room as he squinted his eyes, struggling to read the text on his device.

"13 missed calls." said the message. Taking a deep breath, Graham groaned in frustration as he tapped the screen of his phone to call back.

"What the hell do you want at this ungodly hour?" he inquired, speaking to the caller, his voice coarse and deep from sleep.

"Can't provide an explanation right now, get yourself over to the headquarters ASAP." The man commanded, leaving no time for argument before he hung up.

Frustration as clear as day on Graham's face, he did as told. Pulling into the parking of the Military Intelligence headquarters in London, a sinister and tranquil atmosphere engulfed the city.

The deafening silence of the city in the middle of the night was broken by occasional whooshes of passing-by cars as dim streetlamps enlightened the dark driveway.

Not a soul remained outside, nor a sound except the creaks of crickets invisible to sight. Graham trudged to the main entrance, grappling onto the cold, metal door handle as his breath condensed into a tiny cloud when he took a deep breath, pushing the door open.

Doing so and to his surprise, the headquarters which he expected to appear abandoned were bustling with MI men and police officers in a state of alarm, painting a terrifying picture that something bad is en route.

Walking through the grand corridors he arrived at the Executive, Mr. J.A.Khan's office, who, appeared preoccupied as he fumbled about his chamber juggling bundles of papers and files.

Khan gave a glance at Graham before glancing at the seat facing him, gesturing the man to have a seat as Khan's hands remained tied with papers and his head held up the telephone reciever with shoulder.

"....got it. Yes sir. Morning." with a slam he banged the reciever on the telephone as he shifted his focus to Graham.

"Why the hell am I sitting in your office at two in the morning Khan?" he inquired, his face demanding answers.

"Do you know who is Colonel Gustav Hermann Von Kreig?" asked Khan

"The infamous Nordenheimian Colonel, yes, I am aware. Hasn't he overthrown the government in a coup-d'état?"

"That's right. The man's a modern-day Hitler, Graham," Khan said, his voice heavy with seriousness. "He's not to be taken lightly. He's planning an invasion of several nations in Europe. A spy from the United States just sent us the full list."

Khan turned his laptop 180 degrees so Graham could see for himself. Graham's eyes widened as he scanned the list, then he looked back at Khan in disbelief. "You've got to be kidding me—we're one of them?!"

"Which is why I've decided to send you on a little 'vacation' to Heimstadt to take care of our guy." Khan's tone was firm, but there was a hint of urgency as he rummaged through his desk. "Don't miss your flight," he added, sliding a small envelope toward Graham.

A moment later, Khan's hand emerged from under the desk, gripping a pistol. "Aha. Here it is."

Graham let out a nervous laugh. "You must be mad if you think I'm going to assassinate a dictator right now," he said, but the chuckle quickly faded when he saw the deadly seriousness in Khan's eyes.

"Wait—you're serious about this?"

"Get out of my office."

As Graham approached the door, Khan's voice stopped him. "Also, you aren't Graham Calloway anymore. For the next few weeks you're Ethan Sinclair." he said, tossing Graham a passport and an ID, "Now get going!"

II

Nordenheim

Graham marched to his car, frustrated by the sudden deployment. "Join Military Intelligence, they said," he muttered bitterly, "it'll be fun, they said."

As he pulled into the driveway, a strange sense of unease settled over him, like a pair of unseen eyes were watching, waiting to strike.

Beads of sweat formed on his forehead as his breathing quickened. He gripped his gun tightly, cautiously opening the door.

Standing in front of him was a tall, shadowy figure, its eyes locked onto his.

"Don't come any closer! I-I'll shoot!" he shouted, his voice wavering as he raised the gun.

"You donkey, where have you been at this hour?!" came a familiar voice as the figure stepped into the light.

"Martha?!" Graham exclaimed, his relief turning to disbelief.

"Graham, were you out drinking again?" his wife asked, her tone halfway between scolding and concern.

"What? No, no!" he stammered, lowering his gun. "I just got assigned a mission. I'm leaving for Heimstadt in an hour or so."

“Heimstadt? What is your mission now, to kill that dictator or something?” she asked with an annoyed chuckle.

Graham remained silent, his eyes fixed on the floor, searching for the right words. “Oh, for heaven’s sake, why can’t you have a normal job where you’re not shooting people?” she exclaimed, her tone a mix of worry and frustration.

“Don’t stress over it,” he said, trying to sound reassuring as he gently tapped her shoulder. “This one will be over soon.” He forced a smile before darting toward the bedroom. “Now come on, help me pack. I don’t have all night!

As Graham’s aircraft touched down in Heimstadt early that morning, the state of the airport was a stark reflection of the country’s political instability.

The arrivals section was eerily deserted, occupied only by police officers and a few airport workers. Empty corridors stretched out before him, gate after gate left unoccupied.

In sharp contrast, the departure gates were overwhelmed with crowds desperate to flee. Hundreds, if not thousands, jostled and pleaded at the exits, only to be shoved back by police officers who arrested some in the chaos.

Graham approached the immigration counter, handing over his fake passport. He watched nervously as the official leafed through it, beads of sweat forming on his temples when the officer’s eyes narrowed with scrutiny.

Then, with a swift, practiced motion, the guard stamped the passport and handed it back with a brief smile.

“Welcome to Nordenheim,” he said.

Graham exhaled in relief, stepping out into the cold morning air. He hailed a taxi, blending into the uneasy flow of the city.

As the vehicle slowed to a halt at Schulmann Square, also eerily desolate, Graham couldn’t help but ask, "Why is everything so empty?"

"Curfew sir," replied the driver as he shoved his hand in his pocket, rummaging for change, "they put curfew 9 o’ clock to 18 o‘ clock. You out, they catch, put jail." said the man in broken English, handing back the man his change. "Have nice trip sir."

He said before speeding off, leaving Graham all alone in the desolate, gloomy square.

"Okay... let’s get to business," Graham mumbled as he navigated the deserted streets, stomach growling with hunger.

Spotting a bakery with a half-open shutter and the sign "Bäkeri Heimstadt" overhead, he pushed his way inside, hoping to find something to eat.

Suddenly, the shutter slammed shut behind him, plunging the room into darkness. A sharp, searing pain struck the back of his head, and he crumpled to the floor, stunned but still conscious.

The lights flickered on, revealing a young woman, no older than twenty-five. Her delicate, porcelain-like skin contrasted with her fiery red hair, which seemed to almost glow under the harsh lighting. She stood behind the counter, arms crossed, her face severe and demanding answers.

"What are you doing here?" she barked, her voice thick with a Germanic accent, her piercing green eyes locked onto Graham. A pistol glinted in her right hand, held steady and ready.

"One false move, and I'll blow your brains out," she warned. "Start talking—who sent you here?"

"Okay, first things first," Graham said, raising his hands slowly as he stood up, "you did a terrible job trying to knock me out. All it did was give me a concussion..."

"Sorry, do you *want* me to knock you out for good?" she snapped, raising the gun again, her grip tightening.

"Okay, okay, relax!" he shouted, his hands still up. The woman hesitated, and slowly lowered the barrel of her firearm.

"I'm Ethan Sinclair, British reporter," he explained quickly. "I was just looking for some food!"

The woman lowered her gun even further, studying him for a moment before gesturing toward the counter. "I have all of this. Pick one, and get lost," she commanded, pointing at the assortment of traditional breads lined up in the glass display.

"That one," Graham said, pointing to a cinnamon-filled pastry. Without missing a beat, the woman grabbed it, stuffed it into a paper bag, and rang him up.

"Forty-two Lek ninety-nine," she said, her voice still stern as she held out her hand for the payment.

Graham took the bag and began walking out, but her voice stopped him in his tracks.

"See you later, Graham."

His head whipped around in confusion. "Shut your mouth!" he barked, striding back to the counter. "How do you know my name?!"

The woman didn't flinch. With a casual motion, she reached into her apron and pulled out his ID, holding it up in front of him.

"Maybe I know because I just..." She let the words trail off as she waved the ID in front of him. "...took a little something to see if you were a threat."

Graham's jaw dropped. "How did you—"

"All of that later," she interrupted, tossing the apron aside and untying it. "I know what your mission is, and I want to help you."

She led Graham to a bookshelf, which she pushed open with a swift motion. "Please," she said, gesturing inside a passageway. Hesitant, Graham peeked inside, attempting to see the inside of the dimly-lit passage.

"I'm not trying to kill you," she sneered, "if I wanted to I'd have already done so" with a forceful shove, she pushed him inside and followed, closing the door behind her with a soft thud.

Graham stared, wide-eyed, at what lay before him. Below what had appeared to be an ordinary bakery, an entire underground operation was underway. "What is all of this?" he asked, his voice laced with disbelief.

"This," she said, her voice low but determined, "is my organization, working to overthrow this government."

Around them, men and women sat at desks, glued to their computer screens, while others stood in front of softboards, planning attacks and devising strategies.

"Okay, keep your eyes and ears open," she said, her tone turning serious. "I'm not going to repeat myself." She walked over to a whiteboard, grabbed a marker, and began scribbling furiously. The screech of the marker on the board echoed through the room. "You've got three chances to kill him," she continued, her eyes fixed on the board as she wrote.

"First, he's going to be at a conference in a few days."

She paused, looking up at Graham to gauge his reaction.

"Okay," he said, taking a deep breath, "I have no clue where you're trying to get with *this* little bit of information," he sneered, crossing his arms "you have an entire operation and I have more information than you!"

"Little, eh?" she said, frustrated at Graham's comment and grabbing him by his collar, dragging him to a corner. "I reckon you think this is *little*?" she barked, gesturing to him shelves over shelves stocked with paperwork.

III

The ZEPO

As the sun dipped below the horizon, the city began to quiet down. The busy streets, once filled with people, were now empty and desolate as the curfew hour struck.

Graham and Anna Müller, the woman he had met earlier, continued discussing strategies when their conversation was abruptly interrupted by screams from outside the bakery.

"No, no, please! I have kids at home!" a woman pleaded, her voice filled with terror as she was tackled by men and dragged toward a van.

"We should help her!" Graham shouted, pulling out his weapon, ready to rush to her aid. But Anna yanked him back. "Whoa, whoa, hold on, Superman," she said, gripping his collar firmly. "Not so fast. You think you're trying to be some *hero*?"

"What's going on? Let me save her from those goons!" Graham said, trying to break free from her grasp.

"My friend, those are not goons. Those are the ZEPO" she explained quickly, her voice low but urgent.

"ZEPO? What kind of creature is a ZEPO?" Graham paused, his eyebrows furrowed in confusion.

"Not a creature, you idiot," she sneered, rolling her eyes. "It stands for 'Zekrett Politzki,' Von Kreig's special police."

"You need to get used to all of this," she stated as Graham sat back down, concealing his gun, "there's nothing we can do about this until we defeat the dictator."

As the latter continued the talk, Graham interrupted Anna with a sudden thought, "Wait!" he shouted, "then that means this zedo-"

"ZEPO." she interrupted Graham, correcting him with her tone strong.

"...yeah, that ZEPO thing would also be present with the dictator, we need to do something about this first." he said.

"Hmm, wow, I never thought of that. Thank you," she said, rummaging through her desk for a map.

Graham let out a slight chuckle. "Gee, no problem." His smile faded when she glanced back at him. "You were being sarcastic, weren't you?"

"Anyway," she cleared her throat, "you're going to want to kill this man first." She slid a picture across the desk. "Wilhelm Drexler."

"What's so special about this guy?" Graham asked, still confused.

"Well," she said, leaning forward, "he's the chief of police and also the dictator's aide-de-camp. If you take down Von Kreig, Drexler's coming after you—one hundred percent."

"Oh, great!" he groaned. "Now I have one more person to deal with!"

"Well, you could always take them both out at once if you want to kill two birds with one stone," Anna shrugged. "But I think that might be a bit tricky."

"Tricky? Hard my foot!" he exclaimed. "What's so difficult? I can just shoot one, then take out the other!"

"Before you can shoot the second one, the guards will shoot you," Anna said, her tone flat.

IV

Wilhelm Drexler

As the sun peeked above the horizon, painting the sky in graceful shades of orange and yellow, Graham rose early to meet up with Anna at the bakery.

"Okay," she said, her tone firm, "let's go over the plan." She spread out a map on the table. "Drexler is coming to tour the square. Simple. You see him, you say hi, you put him to sleep for eternity, and then you skedaddle."

Disguised as the British reporter, Graham made his way to the bustling square. The area was teeming with police, a sea of uniforms swarming the overwhelming crowds. Ear-piercing sirens blared in the distance as Drexler's convoy rumbled closer.

The line of vehicles slowed to a stop, and the air tensed as ZEPO agents and police officers disembarked, forming a wall of security. They cleared a path, and Drexler stepped forward, scanning the crowd.

"Okay, you have one chance," Graham thought, gripping the gun tightly. "Do not screw this up."

Feigning interest as a reporter, he edged closer to Drexler, heart pounding in his chest. With a swift movement, he drew the gun. A flash, a deafening bang—and Drexler crumpled to the ground, lifeless.

Chaos erupted. Police lunged for Graham, who spun on his heels, shoving through the panicking crowd. Sirens wailed louder, orders barked through megaphones, but he pushed forward, racing through the frantic square, desperate to evade capture.

Police dogs barked violently, closing in as Graham sprinted for his life. Gunfire cracked behind him, and a sudden, searing pain shot through his right arm—he'd been hit. Ignoring the agony, he ducked into narrow alleyways, weaving through the labyrinth of streets until he finally lost the police.

Staggering back to the bakery, blood dripping from his arm, he burst through the door and tore through the drawers, desperate for a first-aid kit.

Anna's eyes widened at the sight. "Oh my—" she blurted out. "You had one job, and you come back with a bullet in your arm?"

"Shut your mouth and help me bandage this!" Graham snapped, his voice strained with pain as he clenched his arm, the blood pouring faster with every second.

A tense silence settled between them as Anna bandaged Graham's wound. A few minutes later, his bleeding had stopped, and they sat down at a bench with a map sprawled out on the table between them, hurriedly planning the next step.

"Okay," Anna said, wiping her brow. "We don't have a lot of time. The ZEPO will figure out what happened and they'll be at our door in two days, three tops." She tapped the spot where Wilhelm Drexler's tiny figurine lay knocked over on the map.

"Our biggest obstacle is gone, just like that. Now, we focus on the big prize." She circled Von Kreig's figurine, a menacing black piece in the center of the map.

"This isn't going to be as easy as Drexler," she continued, pulling out a small box filled with miniature figurines of soldiers and guards, setting them up around the palace.

"Von Kreig is their top priority, so security will be on another level. This," she said, placing a tiny figure to represent the outer wall, "is our first hurdle—the outer perimeter. Next," she pointed to another set of pieces, "are the security cameras. And here, the patrols—helicopters, and vehicles constantly circling the palace grounds."

Graham's forehead creased in anxiety. "Okay, okay, but I have to ask," he interrupted, leaning forward, "what happens if we get caught?"

Anna didn't miss a beat. "Oh, that's simple!" she replied, her voice detached and almost casual. "He'll make an example out of us—kill us in the slowest and most painful way imaginable."

Graham sat there, stunned, his gaze drifting blankly past Anna for a moment before he found his voice. "That... was quite inspirational to hear," he said with a shaky laugh, trying to mask his nerves. "Anyway, can't I just take him out at the conference you mentioned earlier?"

Anna's face hardened. "No."

"Why not?" he pressed.

"Did you see what happened to you with Drexler and his men?" she shot back, a hint of irritation in her voice. "Drexler wasn't even the most protected man, and yet his security detail nearly killed you! You barely escaped with your life. Now, imagine trying to take out Von Kreig—the most guarded person in the entire country. His men would tear you apart before you even got close."

She leaned forward, her eyes fierce and unyielding. "This isn't a one-man show, Graham. You can't just waltz in guns blazing and hope to get out alive. We need a real plan, and we need to hit him where he least expects it."

V

The Plan

As dawn broke, a calm settled over the city. Birds chirped brightly, and a sweet breeze drifted through the streets, sunlight filtering through cracks in the clouds. The tranquility was shattered by a sudden, violent crash at the bakery's front door, jolting Anna awake.

Grabbing her gun, she crept downstairs, only to come face-to-face with a squad of ZEPO men. A scream escaped her as she bolted out of the bakery, the heavily armed squad hot on her heels.

Mid-sprint, she collided with Graham, who was just on his way to the bakery.

"Anna, what are you doin—" he began, but she cut him off, urgency in her voice. "No time! RUN!"

Together, they dashed through the now-bustling streets, weaving and shoving their way through the growing crowd. People cursed at them in Nordenian, their voices blending into the chaotic noise of the morning.

"What is going on?" Graham shouted, barely able to keep up as they dodged pedestrians and debris.

“The ZEPO! They know!” Anna’s voice was thick with panic.

They rounded a corner and vanished into the crowd, blending seamlessly with the throng. For now, they were safe—hidden in plain sight amidst the busy city.

“How do they know?!” Graham shouted, still panting and flushed from the sprint.

“I don’t know!” Anna replied, her eyes wide in surprise as she wiped sweat from her forehead.

“Well, now we can’t get to the bakery. My operation is completely busted!” Graham threw his hands up in frustration.

“Let’s get to my safehouse,” Anna suggested, her voice steady despite the chaos. “It’s a small apartment, but it’s our last hope.”

Graham nodded, a flicker of determination crossing his face. "Right," he said, taking a seat in a nearby chair. "I think I know what we need to do to get in. It’s not the most conventional, but it’s our best shot."

As the sun dipped below the horizon, the two arrived at the palace gates just as a lieutenant was about to depart.

A swift bonk echoed in the air, followed by a thud as the lieutenant collapsed, unconscious.

"Ow, where am I?" he mumbled groggily, slowly regaining consciousness in the apartment.

Anna stood over him, her expression cold. "Okay, old man," she said firmly, "start talking. Give me every bit of information you have about the security of the palace."

"NO," the lieutenant spat, his voice resolute, refusing to turn his back on the Dictator.

Anna’s eyes narrowed, her patience thinning. "Okay, I see you’re being stubborn," she sneered, glancing at Graham. "My friend will teach you a lesson."

Graham stepped forward, his gun drawn, a cold smile creeping across his face. "Okay, now, are we going to talk, or should I..." he waved the gun in the air menacingly, the threat hanging in the silence.

"Okay, okay, I'm telling!" the lieutenant exclaimed, his resolve crumbling under the weight of the situation.

VI

Einschaft Palace

As night settled over the city, the two sat in silence on the rooftop of the townhouse, the cool breeze brushing their faces. The brightly lit city sprawled before them, with the Square's neon lights flickering in the distance.

"Hey," Graham called out, breaking the stillness. "Why did you start this kind of operation? It's dangerous, and I don't think you've done anything like this before."

Anna let out a deep sigh, her gaze dropping as she searched for the right words. "Before the takeover, I lived with my parents and my younger brother," she began, her voice softening. "When Von Kreig came into power, he arrested everyone from opposition parties and organizations. My parents were big supporters of the opposition."

Her voice faltered for a moment. "They were arrested. I don't know where they are... or if they're even alive." Tears welled in her eyes, but she quickly wiped them away, looking away to compose herself.

Graham was quiet for a beat before asking gently, "What about your brother?"

"He was lucky," she said, her voice stronger now, though tinged with sadness. "He managed to migrate to Stockholm. He lives there now."

"I-I'm sorry for you—" Graham began, but he was quickly interrupted by Anna.

"Don't mention it," she snapped, her tone hardening. "I want to shoot that dog of a ruler the moment I see him!" Her anger was palpable, her clenched fists shaking slightly as she spoke.

"Don't stress it," he reassured, getting up. "I'll get my revenge tomorrow."

As the sun rose over the still city, Graham got ready for the mission.

"Here it is," Anna said, dropping him off a safe distance from the palace. "Don't mess it up, and remember—stick to the plan."

She drove off, leaving Graham alone, the car fading into the distance as he stood, taking a deep breath.

Gathering himself, Graham got to work. Using the lieutenant's intel, he carefully disabled the electric fencing and cut the security cameras, giving himself a clear path. Climbing over the outer security barrier, he moved swiftly and silently.

Turning a corner, he froze—two patrol officers stood guard at the secondary entrance.

His mind raced. Spotting a pebble nearby, he picked it up and tossed it across the yard. The sound was enough; the guards turned and moved away, investigating the noise. Seizing the opportunity, Graham slipped into the palace.

His phone buzzed with a notification: "Use the air vents. They're big enough for you to fit." It was a message from Anna.

Spotting a nearby vent, he pried it open and climbed inside, carefully replacing the grille. Crammed in the narrow, dusty space, he crawled forward, moving stealthily through the palace without a trace.

As he crawled silently through the vents, a burst of laughter echoed below, prompting Graham to inch forward. Carefully, he peered down through the grille, his eyes locking onto his target—Von Kreig, seated at the dining table, laughing and drinking without a care.

Slowly, he began to unscrew the grate, ready to make his move, when suddenly his phone vibrated violently with a series of notifications. He paused, heart racing, and pulled out his phone. It was Anna.

"Stop."

"Stop! Do *not* shoot."

"I'm serious, *do not shoot*!" the messages flashed urgently.

"He's a decoy," Anna typed rapidly. "If you shoot him, the police will be waiting outside the vents. The real Von Kreig is at a conference."

Graham swore under his breath, realizing how close he'd come to blowing it. He tried to shift around in the cramped vent, but it was too tight. Suddenly, he slipped, his body half-falling out of the metal opening. He dangled precariously, twenty feet above the grand hall, directly above the table—mere feet away from the unsuspecting diners.

"Crap, crap, crap!" he whispered frantically, desperately clinging to the vent's edge. His arms strained as he struggled to hoist himself back up, beads of sweat trickling down his face.

Just as he managed to get a firm grip, the grille slipped, hanging by his legs as he teetered on the edge of disaster. With a final burst of effort, he pulled himself back to safety and secured the grate.

"That's it," he thought, breathless. "I'm definitely retiring after this mission. That was way too close."

Crawling out of the vents, Graham moved swiftly toward the rendezvous point where Anna was waiting.

"Stop!" a guard suddenly shouted, spotting him and charging forward. Without hesitation, Graham bolted. In his desperate escape, he threw himself over the electric fence, feeling a sharp jolt as he was briefly zapped. He landed hard on the other side, pain shooting through his limbs as he limped toward Anna's car, which was idling nearby.

"Step on it!" he yelled as he dove into the passenger seat. Tires screeched, and the car sped off, narrowly escaping the guards.

"You told me at the last minute about Von Kreig being a decoy!" Graham growled, frustration evident in his voice. His face was tense, a mixture of anger and disbelief.

"I didn't know until this morning!" Anna shot back, her voice equally tense. "I only got the intel when I dropped you off!"

Graham took a deep breath, trying to calm his racing thoughts. "Fine," he said, his tone softer but still biting. "At least tell me you removed the car's license plates."

Anna's silence was deafening. She cast a nervous glance in his direction, then quickly looked back at the road. A heavy, tense silence filled the car.

"Great!" Graham snapped, his voice dripping with sarcasm. "Now we have to ditch this car!" His frustration boiled over, his tone turning harsh. "I don't even know why I'm still trusting you. Every step of this mission, I've been on my own!"

The duo arrived at the apartment, parking the car hastily before heading upstairs.

"Why is the front door open?" Anna asked, a note of worry creeping into her voice.

"Let's go and find out," Graham said, his brow furrowing.

Pushing the door open, Graham's eyes went wide. "Unbelievable!" he exclaimed. "The lieutenant we captured... he's escaped! We're finished!"

He began pacing, panic bubbling up as he scrambled for a plan. Meanwhile, Anna peered over the balcony, her face going pale as she saw armed men filing into the building below.

"Graham!" she shouted, pulling back. "We need to get out of here now—they're coming up!"

A knock echoed through the apartment, growing heavier and more urgent with each second. "Politzki!" someone barked from outside, the pounding on the door intensifying.

"We have to jump!" Graham yelled, rushing to the balcony. "It's our only shot!"

"Are you insane?" Anna retorted, her voice shaking. "There's no way I'm—"

Before she could finish, Graham took a running leap off the balcony, plummeting five stories down and landing in a trash-filled dumpster with a heavy thud.

Heart pounding, Anna hesitated only for a moment before she followed, landing beside him with a muffled crash. The two of them scrambled out of the dumpster and sprinted to the car, tires screeching as they sped away from the building.

Finding a place to crash for the night, Graham and Anna finally relaxed after the chaos of the evening. While Anna settled into the room, Graham stepped aside to catch up with Khan.

"Are you sure you can trust this woman, Calloway?" Khan's voice was filled with skepticism as Graham recounted the recent events.

"Yes, I'm sure," Graham replied with conviction, though a slight hesitation lingered. "I have a feeling I can trust her."

Khan's tone remained cautious. "Feelings don't count for much here. Don't let your guard down just because she's your partner," he warned. "You can't trust anyone in this country."

Unbeknownst to Graham, back at the ZEPO headquarters, a team of men listened intently to every word, intercepting the call.

"Mr. Drexler," one of the men called out, "we have them. We've got the entire conversation."

"Excellent," Drexler said, a satisfied smile spreading across his face. "Keep monitoring them. I'll give you further instructions soon."

As Graham ended the call and returned to the room, he found Anna hunched over her laptop, her eyes glued to the screen.

"What are you doing?" Graham asked, startling her.

"Oh!" Anna jumped, stuttering slightly, "N-nothing. I was just... really caught up in this movie." She forced a smile, but her nervousness was evident.

VII

From Anonymous,

As the sun rose over the city, Graham and Anna started preparing a new plan.

"They're obviously much smarter than we anticipated," Anna said, rubbing her chin as she searched for a strategy. "I don't know how to move forward from here."

A knock at the door interrupted her thoughts. "Oh, man, not again!" Graham groaned, bracing himself to run.

"Hey, hey, hey!" Anna said, grabbing him by the collar to stop him. "Relax, it's just Czeslaw."

"It's who?" Graham asked, puzzled.

"Czeslaw. One of the guys from my agency," she replied in an almost exasperated tone. "Just call him Chez. He's not going to bite."

Anna pulled open the door, revealing a man holding a thick file. He walked in without saying much, and he and Anna exchanged a few words in Nordenian. After a moment, Czeslaw dropped the file off and left.

"What did... Chez give you?" Graham asked, eyeing the file warily.

"Oh, it's nothing," Anna said dismissively, walking over to the file. "Probably just some new intel for the mission."

Graham opened the file, and as his eyes scanned the pages, a chill ran down his spine.

"ANNA, RUN!" he shouted, grabbing her by the arm and yanking her toward the door.

"What's wrong with you?!" she shouted in frustration, stumbling in his wake.

Graham's heart pounded as he looked back, eyes wide with panic. "I thought there was a bomb—"

Before he could finish, a deafening bang filled the air, followed by a blinding burst of yellow light that erupted from the windows of their apartment.

Anna's face twisted with fury as she shook free of Graham's grip. "I swear, if I ever see Czeslaw again—"

The explosion sent them both into a sprint, debris raining down around them as they fled the building. Anna's hands were clenched into tight fists, her eyes wild with a mix of rage and disbelief.

"How could he—?" she muttered to herself.

Graham, still processing what had just happened, could only shake his head. "We can't trust anyone anymore. This whole thing is falling apart."

Anna glanced at him, her face tight with determination. "We don't have time to figure out why he did it. We need to get out of here—now."

As the two scurry from the explosion site, loud chants of civilians were audible in a distance. Curious, Anna and Graham followed the source of the sound, reaching to an all-out civil unrest.

Violent riots erupted as the crowd chanted, overwhelming the riot police, who were being beaten on all fronts.

"Well, I think this should be more than enough to stop Von Kreig," Graham said, watching the chaos unfold. "*I'm* heading back to London!"

"Get over here, you," Anna sneered, grabbing him by the arm. "Bet you a million bucks, they'll be knocked over like bowling pins by the ZEPO."

As predicted, the ZEPO arrived with military precision. Armed with anti-riot weapons and fire engines, they blasted high-pressure water at the rioters, while tear gas and rubber bullets slowed the crowd's advance.

Graham and Anna sat on the sidewalk, having nowhere to seek shelter, when suddenly, Graham's phone buzzed, complicating the mission further.

An unknown number.

"I am an ex-member of Von Kreig's regime and a close confidant. I am no longer in Nordenheim; I was one of the lucky few to escape. I can help you—trust me with the intel I'm about to send."

"Who are you?" Graham asked, concealing the texts from Anna. "How did you get my number?" He typed, confusion and suspicion creeping into his thoughts.

"What's that you've got there, Graham?" Anna asked, attempting to peek at his phone.

"Oh, uh, it's nothing," he stammered, jumping slightly. "J-just me and my wife talking... yeah, just her..." he mumbled nervously, feeling the sweat building on his palms.

The phone buzzed again. Graham's heart skipped a beat as the new message appeared on the screen.

"Von Kreig's real residence is not Einschaft Palace," the message read. "His true residence is unknown. Only his top men and personal soldiers know the location."

"Then where has Anna been leading me for the past few days?" Graham thought to himself, his mind racing with doubt and suspicion. Each passing second, his mistrust toward Anna grew stronger.

Anna seemed preoccupied as she glanced at Graham, a frown forming on her face. “I just found out from someone that they say Von Kreig lives somewhere unknown, but his true residence *is* in Einschaft Palace!”

Graham froze, his thoughts racing. "These pieces of information are contradicting," he thought to himself, feeling a rising sense of urgency. "I must choose to follow only one; the other is a trap."

Before he could decide, Anna’s voice broke his concentration. “Listen,” she began, but Graham cut her off.

“No,” he spat, his voice cold and firm. “This time, we’re going by my plan.”

The moment the words left his mouth, Anna’s demeanor shifted. She became visibly nervous, trying to persuade him to go along with her idea.

“I said no!” Graham snapped again, his tone leaving no room for argument. “We’re going to an auction where a device is being sold. The device was previously owned by Von Kreig and is said to contain important information.”

Reluctantly, Anna agreed. Disguised as wealthy businesspeople, Graham and Anna made their way to the underground auction. The location reeked of secrecy, and the basement had an air of illicit dealings.

“Welcome, ladies and gentlemen, to the auction of this beautiful device,” the auctioneer announced, his voice bright and confident as he held up the device for all to see. “Supposedly owned previously by Gustav Hermann Von Kreig.”

“We are starting the bidding at fifty thousand Leks!” he continued.

“One hundred thousand,” a voice called out.

"Two hundred thousand," another bidder shouted.

"Seven hundred thousand!" came another.

"One million!" yet another voice joined in, raising the stakes.

Anna whispered to Graham, her voice laced with disbelief, "Is this piece of trash really worth that much?"

"Shh," Graham whispered back, his eyes locked on the device. He raised his hand. "One and a half million!"

"Wait a minute—that's Calloway!" someone shouted, turning the attention to Graham.

"GET HIM!" another voice yelled, and suddenly, guns were drawn from all sides.

"Drop your weapons!" a group of armed men shouted, equally ready to fight.

"Uh-oh..." Anna muttered, her eyes widening in realization. "This is about to get ugly..."

Graham quickly barked an order. "Run!" he shouted, and the two of them sprinted away as the room erupted into chaos, the sound of gunfire filling the air.

"WHY ARE THOSE MEN TRYING TO KILL YOU?!" Anna yelled as they darted through the maze of corridors, gunshots ringing out behind them.

Graham shot back, narrowly missing a few of the attackers. "Turns out," he panted, trying to keep pace, "I've pissed off a lot of people during my previous missions."

"WHAT?!" Anna exclaimed, a mix of confusion and fear in her voice.

"One of them's a Colombian cartel," Graham continued, his breathing heavy from running. "The other's a Brazillian gang!"

As the duo continued sprinting through the streets, the cartel now hot on their trail, they found themselves at a dead end.

"I think this is what they call a 'dead end'!" Anna exclaimed, her voice laced with fear as she glanced back at the approaching men.

"Quick, down the gutter!" Graham shouted, lifting the manhole cover with urgency.

The cartel members, relentless in their pursuit, descended after them into the dark, dank tunnel, turning on their searchlights as they waded through knee-deep murky water.

Anna and Graham, barely audible in the darkness, moved swiftly into a shadowy nook, watching the cartel men run past them, oblivious to their presence. Once the danger had passed, they climbed back up to street level, their clothes soaked and their hearts racing.

After checking into a nearby hotel, they collapsed into a dim, musty room. Graham pulled out his phone, his nerves on edge as it buzzed with a series of incoming messages from the same anonymous number. His hands shook slightly as he unlocked the screen.

"ARE YOU MAD?"

The next message followed quickly: *"DO AS I TELL YOU IF YOU DO NOT WANT TO BE MURDERED BY A GANG."*

Graham's brow furrowed as he read the warning. The implications hit him hard. He glanced at Anna, who was unpacking, unaware of the conversation happening on his phone.

A nagging thought gnawed at him. Could the anonymous person be the one pulling the strings? Or was Anna the one working against him all along? He hadn't told her about the messages yet. Too much had happened in too short a time, and the truth was, he didn't know who to trust anymore.

Anna suddenly spoke, pulling him from his thoughts. "What is it?" she asked, glancing over at him. "Why are you looking at your phone like that?"

Graham quickly pocketed the device, his expression a mask of calm. "Nothing," he said, trying to sound nonchalant. "Just some updates from our contacts."

Anna seemed to buy it, nodding and walking over to the window. She pushed the curtains aside, surveying the street below. "We need to figure out our next move," she muttered. "We can't stay here for long. The cartel won't stop until they find us."

Graham's mind raced. The more he thought about the anonymous messages, the more questions piled up. He was being warned, but by whom? Was it a genuine ally, or was he being manipulated?

He glanced at Anna, who was still looking out the window, her face tense. Should he tell her? Could he trust her? He didn't know what to think anymore.

He typed a response to the anonymous number: "Who are you? Why should I trust you?"

Just as he hit send, the door to their room suddenly creaked. Graham's body tensed, and Anna spun around, hand on the gun tucked into the waistband of her pants. But it was only a knock.

"Who is it?" Anna called out, her voice controlled but her posture alert.

A muffled voice responded from the other side. "It's me. Czeslaw."

Graham's gaze shifted to Anna, his mind racing. Should they let him in? Could this be a setup? If Anna had anything to do with it, they might be walking into yet another trap.

Anna hesitated but then moved toward the door. She cracked it open just enough to peek through.

Czeslaw stood outside, his expression grave, his hands clutching a thick file. His eyes flicked from Anna to Graham, and then he leaned in, lowering his voice. "We need to talk. *Now*."

Anna hesitated, then stepped aside, letting Czeslaw in.

Graham didn't react immediately. He was too busy weighing the options in his head. Anna? Czeslaw? The anonymous messages?

He wasn't sure anymore. But one thing was certain: Someone was playing them. And he wasn't sure who to trust.

"Czeslaw, you son of a mangy dog!" Anna shouted, her face flushed with anger as she lunged at him, fists clenched. "YOU ALMOST MURDERED US!"

"What? *NO!*" Czeslaw stammered, stepping back, his face paling. "The file I brought was switched on the bus! Yes, I remember! A woman carrying the same kind of file bumped into me! I think she must've switched it then."

Anna paused, her fists still raised, staring at him in disbelief. "Are you serious?" she spat, her voice dripping with suspicion. "You expect me to believe that?"

Czeslaw held up his hands, palms outward, a gesture of surrender. "I swear! I had no idea that file was dangerous. I'm not working against you!"

The room was thick with tension as Anna eyed him warily. Graham stood silent, his gaze flicking between the two of them. He was thinking, processing the information. Could this be the truth? Was he being lied to again?

Just as the argument between Anna and Czeslaw reached its peak, Graham's phone buzzed again, vibrating harshly in his pocket. He pulled it out quickly, eyes narrowing as he read the new message:

"Do not trust Czeslaw."

His heart skipped a beat. He looked up at Anna and Czeslaw, both of them still shouting at each other. The weight of the message settled heavily on his chest.

"What's wrong?" Anna asked, noticing the change in his expression. "You look like you've seen a ghost."

Without responding, Graham glanced down at the screen again, as if the words might change or reveal something more. But no—there it was, clear and direct: "Do not trust Czeslaw."

Anna noticed Graham's unease. "Who's that from?" she asked, trying to peek over his shoulder.

Graham quickly locked the phone and shoved it back into his pocket. "Just... nothing important," he muttered, his mind racing.

He couldn't shake the nagging feeling that someone was playing both sides. Was Czeslaw genuinely innocent, or was he part of the trap? What if the anonymous messages were true? His instincts screamed that he couldn't afford to make the wrong choice now.

VIII

Republic of Rostovia

"Hey," said Czeslaw, popping back into the room, "I forgot to tell you—there are some important documents in a nearby data center. Allegedly, they include the blueprint and address of Von Kreig's real home. Anna, I'll send you the location." With that, he walked out, slamming the door behind him.

Moments later, Anna's phone buzzed. She had received the coordinates for the data center, a place far away from the bustling city. As Anna and Graham began discussing their strategy, Graham's phone rang.

"Sorry," he said, standing up, "I need to take this. It's important."

It was the anonymous user again.

"The documents are *supposedly* in the data center," the message read. "But I've heard they were destroyed—burnt to ashes."

Graham's pulse quickened. He was now at a crossroads, forced to decide between trusting Anna or the mysterious messenger.

Before Graham could respond to the anonymous message, Anna suddenly grabbed his arm, her eyes intense and sincere.

"Look, Graham," she said, her voice steady, "I know you have doubts, and I don't blame you. But I've put everything on the line to be here with you. If I was playing you, I wouldn't have risked my life back there in the alley *or* at that auction. You *saw* how close we got to dying."

"What do you mean?" He asked, surprised, his eyes twitching nervously since Anna was not aware of the messages

"I have a feeling that your trust for me is fraying," she said, "you've been acting strange and hesitant around me."

She paused, taking a deep breath before pulling out a small, worn-out photograph from her jacket pocket. "This was my brother," she said softly, her voice breaking a little. "He tried to expose Von Kreig years ago and vanished without a trace. I'm in this to finish what he started...and I need you to believe me, Graham. I have no one else I trust."

Graham felt a knot tighten in his stomach. Anna's raw emotion was something he couldn't fake, and her determination seemed real—so real it almost hurt to doubt her. He found himself wavering, torn between the anonymous warnings and the genuine plea from the person right in front of him.

As Graham sat back down and continued brainstorming, a sudden thought struck him. Hadn't she said her brother escaped to Sweden as a refugee? His pulse quickened.

Her stories have so many gaps...

"Where are you wandering off to?" Anna asked, noticing Graham's distant look.

"Oh—no, nothing," he stammered. "I was just thinking about what you said earlier, that your brother escaped to Sweden," he continued, trying to sound casual. "But now you're saying he disappeared a while ago."

Her face visibly paled, and a flicker of panic crossed her features. After a few seconds of tense silence, she responded, "Well, I—I have two brothers," she said, forcing a nonchalant tone, but the nervousness was clear in her eyes.

Graham's gaze narrowed as he caught the slight tremor in her voice and the way she avoided his gaze. A heavy silence settled between them.

"Two brothers?" he repeated skeptically. "Funny you never mentioned a second one before."

Anna forced a weak smile, her fingers fidgeting with the corner of a photograph she held. "It just... never came up," she said with a shrug that felt too casual. "My family is complicated. We don't exactly have reunions, you know?"

Graham's instincts told him something wasn't right, but he decided to push the thought aside. Now wasn't the time to press her—not when they had bigger problems to face.

"Alright," he said slowly, doubt still gnawing at him.

Disguised as guards, Graham and Anna arrived at the data center, ready to steal the crucial documents. Their car slowed to a stop in front of the main entrance, where a group of guards, speaking in rapid Nordenian, surrounded them.

After a tense exchange of words, the guards grudgingly stepped aside, opening the gates and allowing the vehicle to pass through.

"Now," Graham said, pulling out a keycard he had stolen from another officer, "we just have to use this."

They approached the data center's entrance. Graham swiped the keycard, and a bright beep sounded as the heavy doors creaked open.

"We're the data observers," Anna told a nearby guard, keeping her voice steady. "We'll be quick, just need to check some documents in Vault Seven."

The guard eyed them skeptically, demanding an ID or keycard. Graham handed over the card, holding his breath as the guard inspected it carefully.

"Come," the guard finally said, signaling for them to follow.

They arrived at the vault—a towering, steel door several feet thick. The guard punched a passcode into the keypad, and with a deep, metallic groan, the vault door swung open.

The guard said something in Nordenian, his gaze fixed on them.

"He's saying he has to stand by and watch us work," Anna whispered to Graham, leaning in nervously.

"I've got an idea..." Graham muttered, beckoning the guard closer.

Without hesitation, Graham swung the butt of his rifle, knocking the guard unconscious. "Out cold, just like that!" he said, grinning down at the slumped figure. "Didn't think a rifle-butt could be so handy!"

They moved quickly, stuffing documents into their bags, urgency mounting. But as they turned to leave, the guard stirred. Before they could react, he discreetly pressed an alarm button.

Suddenly, red lights flashed, sirens blared, and the heavy vault door swung shut.

"No, no, NO!" Anna shouted, banging her fists against the thick metal.

"We're locked in!" she said, panic rising in her voice as the alarms drowned out her words.

"Relax! I know how to get us out of here!" Graham reassured, pulling Anna back from the vault door.

Just then, the door began to creak open, revealing an armed squad of ZEPO men, weapons raised, ready to neutralize the intruders.

Hiding behind a stack of filing cabinets, Anna and Graham held their breath, waiting for the right moment. When the guards turned their attention away for a split second, the two slipped out, moving like shadows.

But they weren't completely unnoticed. Shouts erupted behind them, and soon a chase ensued, the roar of engines echoing through the steep mountain roads.

"What do we do?!" Graham shouted, his voice edged with panic, as he swerved along the narrow curves. In the rearview mirror, the ZEPO vehicles were gaining, their lights flashing ominously.

"Let's escape the country!" Anna yelled over the roar of the engine.

"WHAT?!" Graham's eyes darted from the road to Anna, his voice full of disbelief.

"See that flagpost?" she said, pointing to a distant red flag fluttering on the mountainside. "Once we cross that line, we'll be in the Republic of Rostovia! The ZEPO has no jurisdiction there—we'll be safe!"

With no other choice, Graham pressed the gas pedal harder, speeding towards the border. They tore across the rugged terrain, the car skidding dangerously around bends. Just as they passed the red flag, the ZEPO vehicles screeched to a sudden halt, unable to pursue any further.

Breathless, Graham and Anna exchanged a look of relief. They had made it—barely.

"That was CRAZY!" Anna shouted, her breaths ragged as the adrenaline began to fade.

"I think it's time to ditch the car," Graham said, scanning the horizon. "It won't be long before the Rostovian guards catch up and try to send us back. We'll have to sneak into Nordenheim from the mountains—the ZEPO will be waiting for us at the official border."

They abandoned the car, scrambling up the steep slopes until they crossed back over the line of red flags, re-entering Nordenheim. Exhausted, Anna slumped onto a rock, unzipping her bag.

"Alright, let's see what we managed to grab," she said, rifling through the documents.

Her face fell. "Oh, come on!" she groaned. "We got everything except what we actually needed!"

Just then, Graham's phone buzzed, the screen lighting up with a new message from Anonymous.

"Neat escape there," it read.

His blood ran cold as he stared at the screen. "I told you those documents weren't there."

A shiver ran down his spine. How did this mysterious person know every move they made?

"Who is this?" Anna demanded, catching Graham off guard as he quickly tried to shield his phone.

"I—I don't know," he stammered, his voice defensive. "It's probably nothing. Just let it go."

But Anna wasn't buying it. With a swift motion, she snatched the phone from his grasp, her eyes darting over the messages. Her expression shifted from curiosity to alarm, her face paling as she read.

"I don't want you talking to this person," she said, her tone wavering between scolding and fear. "You have no idea who they are—it could be someone from the ZEPO, for all we know."

She returned the phone after clearing the chats, her expression unreadable.

The two of them continued their journey and, after a long day of relentless walking, finally decided to check into a hotel for the night.

Graham sank into the bed, exhausted, and stared blankly at his phone. He opened the chatroom with the anonymous user, noticing there hadn't been any new messages since Anna had cleared the previous ones.

His eyelids began to flutter, the fatigue catching up with him, when suddenly, the top of the chat changed to "typing." Graham's heart skipped a beat as his eyes snapped open.

"I know you don't trust me, nor does Anna," the message read.

"But I know why she's acting strange."

"I am her brother. I live in Stockholm. Something told me she started working for Von Kreig, which led me to contact you. I'm not completely sure, but be careful. Don't follow her anywhere suspicious."

As morning broke, Graham woke up early, the weight of the stolen documents pressing on his mind. He was trying to formulate an assassination plan using the information he'd gathered. His fingers sifted through the papers when a buzz on his phone interrupted his thoughts.

"Anna will try to lead you into the Einschaft Palace under the pretense of looking for more documents," the message read. "DO NOT GO THERE. There is a bunker designed for Von Kreig in the palace. Hide there. Do as I say if you don't want to be killed by the guards, already planning so in a shooting. Anna is NOT trustworthy."

His heart pounded as he glanced over at Anna, who was still asleep, her breathing slow and steady. The message felt like a slap in the face.

"Why?" he typed, his fingers trembling slightly as he demanded an explanation.

"Good luck," came the response, and then the chat was cleared.

IX

The Fatal Mistake

Anna stirred awake, unaware of the messages Graham had exchanged with the anonymous user. She stretched, then walked over to the desk, flipping through the scattered documents. "Come on, Graham," she said with a spark of enthusiasm, "I've heard that the documents we need are in a vault at Einschaft Palace. Once we have them, we can finally take down Von Kreig!"

Graham hesitated, his stomach knotting with unease. "No," he said firmly, shaking his head. "Let's find another way. Breaking into that palace again is too dangerous."

Anna paused, her expression softening. "Oh no," she said, her voice tinged with concern, "did that anonymous garbage start feeding you lies about me again?"

"What? No, no!" Graham replied hastily, setting his phone face down on the table. "It's just... I don't think this is the right move. It's too risky."

Anna sighed, stepping closer to him, her eyes resolute. "Graham, I am not a traitor. I want to avenge what they did to my parents. This is the only way. Without you, I can't do it. Please, I need your help."

Her voice softened as she pleaded, "The anonymous person is lying. I would never betray you."

After a long pause, Graham exhaled deeply. "Okay," he said, reluctantly nodding. "I'll come. What's the plan?"

Anna's face lit up with relief. "In short: we break in, grab the documents, and scurry out before they know we're there," she said, determination radiating from her.

Czeslaw, their getaway driver, pulled the car to a halt near the outskirts of Einschaft Palace. "I'll meet you both here in two hours," he said before speeding off, the hum of the engine fading into the distance.

Anna turned to Graham, her expression firm. "You know the drill—cut the security."

Graham nodded, skillfully severing the palace's power supply. The entire compound plunged into darkness, allowing the duo to slip past the gates unnoticed.

"That was... easier than I thought," Graham whispered, surprised by the smooth entry.

Anna smirked as they reached the vault deep within the palace. "This is it," she said, crouching by the keypad. Her fingers worked quickly, and after an hour of tense concentration, a soft beep signaled her success. The vault door groaned as it swung open, revealing rows of shelves laden with documents.

"So, the anonymous person was lying," Graham thought as he picked up a blueprint labeled Von Kreig's Residence. Relief washed over him as he examined it.

As they sifted through the shelves, footsteps echoed faintly behind them. Before they could react, the lights snapped back on, and a group of armed men emerged from the shadows of the vault itself, weapons raised and blocking the exit.

"RUN!" Graham shouted, yanking Anna away from the shelves. The guards didn't fire—they wanted them alive—but that only added to the danger.

"No way out!" Anna cried, her voice trembling as they skidded to a halt in the middle of the room.

Graham's mind raced. Then he remembered: The bunker! He'd seen its location in the documents. "The bunker—it's outside the vault!" he said, pulling her toward the back of the room.

The two dodged between shelves, weaving past the advancing guards. Bursting out of the vault, they sprinted down a narrow hall as shouts followed close behind.

"There!" Graham spotted the hidden hatch embedded in the floor. He wrenched it open and dove in, dragging Anna after him. The heavy hatch slammed shut just as the guards reached the hallway, their yells muffled by the thick steel.

Breathing heavily, Anna looked around at the dimly lit space below. "What... is this place?"

"The bunker," Graham said grimly. "Von Kreig's escape route. We'll figure it out from here."

"Graham," Anna said, her brows furrowed in concern as she stepped closer. "I think there's something on your neck..." Her voice trailed off, her eyes squinting as though trying to get a better look.

"What is it?" Graham asked, his hand instinctively moving to touch the spot.

As Anna leaned in closer, Graham felt a sudden, sharp pain. His hand shot up to his neck, where he found the cold steel of a syringe embedded in his skin. The plunger was fully depressed.

"Anna—" he managed to stammer before his vision blurred. His legs gave way, and he crumpled to the floor, unconscious.

When he stirred, the harsh glare of overhead lights pierced his eyes. He was propped against a cold, damp wall, his muscles weak and unresponsive. His head throbbed, but his instincts flared to life as he heard footsteps echoing in the distance.

Several figures entered the room. As his vision focused, his stomach sank.

"Neat trick, wasn't it?" said a familiar voice.

It was Anna.

Graham's eyes widened in disbelief. Behind her, Drexler and Von Kreig stood, their faces twisted into triumphant smirks.

"It's—It's not possible!" Graham sputtered, his voice shaky but furious. He pointed at Drexler, his hand trembling. "I killed you! I watched you die!"

Drexler chuckled, the sound low and menacing. "And yet, here I am. A pity, really, for an 'experienced' agent to be so clueless about body doubles. Tsk, tsk, poor boy."

Graham's gaze snapped back to Anna, betrayal and rage flooding his expression. "Who are you?" he demanded, his voice laced with venom.

Anna smiled—a cruel, mocking smile. "Hildegard Drexler," she said with icy precision. "Daughter of Wilhelm Drexler." She paused, watching his shock turn to horror. "It's almost laughable how easily we fooled you."

"YOU TRAITOR!" Graham roared, his voice echoing in the bunker. The truth hit him like a sledgehammer: the close calls, her distracted behavior, the cryptic warnings from the anonymous user.

It had all been a trap.

Hildegard's smile only widened. "Oh, Graham," she said, her voice dripping with mock sympathy. "You never stood a chance."

"Get this squirm out of my hair. Immediately," Von Kreig commanded, his voice dry with sympathy.

He and his entourage left without a backward glance, the heavy door slamming shut behind them.

Just as the soldiers cocked their rifles, Graham's phone buzzed weakly in his hand. His fading strength allowed him to glance at the screen one last time.

"I was forced. I am sorry."
–Anonymous

Graham's grip on the phone slackened as a bitter smile crept onto his face. "Forced or not, it's all the same now," he whispered under his breath, "how was I so stupid?"

Before it all finished for Graham, with every ounce of his remaining strength he managed to type out one final message to Khan.

"Mission failed."

The soldiers raised their weapons, and the faint glow of the screen faded in the cold bunker light.

www.ingramcontent.com/pod-product-compliance
Lightning Source LLC
La Vergne TN
LVHW091238150826
845673LV00003B/1204

* 9 7 9 8 8 9 6 3 2 1 6 9 9 *